The Adventures of Shelley Crabster
& The New Pink Shell

Written by Kim Johnson • Illustrated by Mara Davis

Copyright © 2015 Kim Johnson
All rights reserved
Shelley Crabster is a trademark of
Inspired Girl Productions

ISBN-13:978-0692540046
ISBN-10:0692540040

To my Mom...I miss you
everyday.
I hope the adventure
you are on now
is everything you knew
it would be.
I love you more than
words can express.

~Kim

To Xander, Adalyn,
McKenna, Emma & Liam:

May you always have
the strength,
courage and support
you need to
follow your hearts
and live your dreams!

~Mara

Parent Guide

Everyone dreams. Some dream big and some not so much; whatever the scope, they are all important. Children jump in and out of their dream world very easily. They live in it moment to moment. They take so much joy from their imagination and wonder and they are happy to share it with everyone around them.

As the adults in their lives, how we interact with them as they share those dreams with us is of the utmost importance. If we give them our opinions when they share their thoughts, we must be extremely careful with our words and intensity. To a child, especially a small child who has yet to form a strong identity for himself, harsh or poorly thought out reactions can alter the course of his life.

Often in my coaching sessions, I work with parents to help them understand their children and how to create the best environment for them to thrive in. Connecting and communicating with enthusiasm and love matters. In my opinion, it is one of the most critical elements built into a thriving child and home.

When I was a small child, I would come home from kindergarten and immediately want to play school. I would line up my dolls, teddy bears and stuffed animals to act as students. Vivid memories flood my mind with sheer joy of when my parents gave me a chalkboard! Each student had a name and an assigned seat. I would pass out lessons, write on my beautiful chalkboard and create in bliss for hours every day.

My parents thought this was cute. For me, it was so much more. I had wanted to be a teacher for as long as I could remember. My conversations revolved around "playing school" and "writing papers" each and every day.

This was my entire elementary world. Once I met my second grade teacher, Mrs. Walker, it was a done deal. I was going to be a teacher. When I shared this with my father, who I adored and idolized, he was not exactly supportive. He smiled and told me "Well, maybe." At the time, I didn't fully understand. As time progressed, I would share my dream again and again. He would always be less than excited. Then, finally, one day, he informed me that being a teacher would not make me enough money and that I should be planning for something that makes me money. I had no idea what that really meant. I just knew that he didn't seem very happy with my choice...and that changed me as well as what I chose for my life.

I am sharing this story with you so you can understand that comments, even innocent comments, impact our children. How we say something and what we say, can affect whether or not our children hang on to their dreams.

Dreams are the road map of our growing and expanding souls. We begin creating dreams for ourselves very early in our lives. These initial dreams may seem simplistic and small, maybe even unimportant or insignificant, but make no mistake, they are not. It is our duty as the guardians of our children, that we hold their dreams dear. We need to make sure we do what is right by this blessing.

The best way to encourage your child's dreams is to talk about them. Ask questions. Get details. Show enthusiasm! Let them see you smile when talking with them about their dreams. Children are always living in the present moment. When we engage them by asking for details and showing genuine interest, we are practicing genuine connection with them. These are the magic moments. This type of connection feels wonderful for adults and really allows children to feel you "get them".

This can take practice! Be patient with yourself. Often, we are so used to telling our children what to do or asking questions only about school, we forget about their thoughts and dreams. No matter how silly or distracting their dreams may seem to us in the moment, find space for them anyway.

As you read this book with your child, remember your own dreams, remember the ones you may have given up. Do you remember an adult that showed genuine interest when you were small? One who encouraged you to dream and live that dream? For me, that was my Aunt Irene. She was a real character and in her 70's when I was about six years old. She would dream with me and always told me not to listen to anyone, encouraging me to eat dessert first and have fun. I adored her and her blue Volkswagen Beetle.

No matter what your approach, this process is about acceptance and connection. I hope you have as much fun with Shelley Crabster and her friends as Mara and I did creating her!

KEEP DREAMING & LIVING THOSE DREAMS!

Kim

I grew up on a white sand beach in an ordinary brown shell with many crabs just like me.

Everything there was beautiful.
Our beach was the only place we had ever been or could ever remember being.

Everyone seemed very happy.

Each day was the same.
We all looked the same and did the same things every day: searching for food, trading shells and crawling around the beach and water. It was all the same.

I wanted something
I wanted something new.

Ever since I can remember, I had always wondered what was beyond the beach. I wondered what it was like to fly like the birds. I wondered what new friends I could make. Most of all, I wondered what it would be like to have a bright pink shell!

No matter what I did, my mind was always  about what else was out beyond our beach, and about my new pink shell.

I would imagine my shell had sparkles and a beautiful swirl down the middle. I could see myself dancing and snapping my claws above my head, doing a happy crabby dance and wearing my new shell.

Whenever I would tell my friends and family about my wonderful new shell, they would laugh at me. Almost everyone told me I was crazy. I would hear...

But somehow I felt this was not true.

My heart just knew that my new shell was somewhere waiting for me. Everyday I would climb the highest rock on the jetty and look out over the ocean and dream.

Just when I started to think that maybe they were right,
I heard a voice say to me...

Where are you thinking of going?

I looked over and there was a big, beautiful seagull standing behind me.

Now as a hermit crab, I should be very afraid of seagulls. You see, they eat crabs! But this seagull was different. He wanted to be my

friend.

We started to talk, and talk, and talk.
Gus, that was his name, shared all his flying

adventures

with me.

He told me about all the whales, dolphins and turtles he knew.

He told me about bright blue waters and sparkling sunsets.

He told me about all of the adventures he had been on in his life.

Before I could even ask him, Gus told me about a beach that had pink sand and all different colors of shells!

I was **overjoyed!**

Could my very own pink shell be on that beach? It all sounded so beautiful and exactly like

I had imagined it to be!

As I shared Gus's stories with everyone else on the beach, they were all stunned. All I would hear was...

"How can she be friends with him?"

"He is not telling her the truth."

I knew differently.

I knew my new shell was waiting for me on the pink sand beach!

So the very next time I saw Gus, I asked him to take me to the pink sand beach.

I climbed on his back and off

we flew!

As I looked down, I saw everyone looking up at Gus and me flying away. They were all yelling, "You'll see," but I trusted myself and Gus too, so off we flew.

We flew over the jetty and the ocean, and above the jumping dolphins, before I saw the beach off in the distance.

The sand was so pink! It was so
beautiful!

As we landed I noticed that there were shells everywhere. Just then I saw my pink one! It was waiting for me, as if it had my name on it, waiting for me to discover it.

I just couldn't believe my eyes. It was so special! More so than I had ever

imagined!

I jumped right out of my brown shell and into the new pink one. It was the perfect fit!

I began to do my

happy

crabby

dance

just as I had imagined.

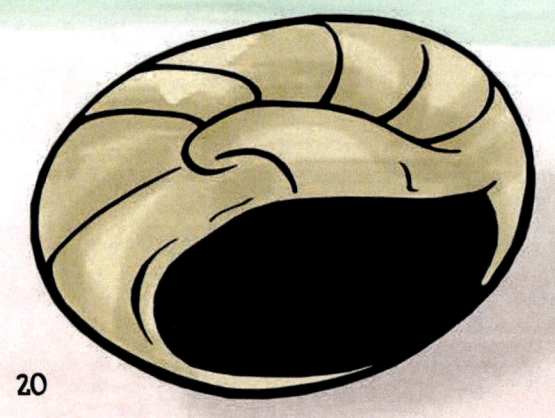

My heart was singing!

Gus and I laughed and had fun the entire day while we made friends with all the new creatures who lived on the pink sand beach.

When Gus said it was time to go, everyone asked me to stay there with them.

My heart just leaped.

"Yes! Yes!", I screamed.

But first I had to go back and tell everyone about my

adventure.

Gus flew me with my new shell back to the white sand beach. I told everyone about my new friends and showed them my new shell.

Some seemed happy for me. Others seemed jealous. Others just walked away from me. But I didn't care.

I knew in my heart that I had to trust myself and remember what my grandfather, Sherman Crabster, had told me.

He said, "Some creatures will laugh at you, some creatures will be jealous of you and some creatures will ignore you. The only thing that matters is what you believe about yourself, in your heart, and that you trust yourself.

Your heart

is where your true answers come from.

So I listened to my heart and said my goodbyes to everyone on the white sand beach.

I went back to the pink sand beach where Gus and I have **adventures** all the time and I live in my beautiful pink shell, doing the happy crabby dance all the time!

Made in the USA
Middletown, DE
06 November 2015